For Jane and Sam.

A.McA.

For my beautiful wife, Linda, and crazy, wonderful children, Albie, Flossie and Lillie.

"Wherever they are, there is Eden."

Also for Julie who, through her teaching, inspired so many children.

G.B.S.

ANGELA McALLISTER

LEON AND THE PLACE BETWEEN

GRAHAME BAKER-SMITH

templar publishing

BIG

MAGIC
SHOW
TONIGHT

"I DON'T BELIEVE IN
MAGIC,"
said Tom, as he settled on the grass in the show tent.
Around him the crowd waited impatiently for
SOMETHING TO HAPPEN.
"IT'S NOT REAL," hissed Pete. "IT'S ONLY TRICKS."
Little Mo looked disappointed.
"SSSH NOW," whispered their brother
LEON.
"IT WILL BE MAGIC. YOU HAVE TO BELIEVE.
LOOK, IT'S GOING TO BEGIN."

THE LANTERNS WENT OUT.
In the darkness the crowd fidgeted with excitement. There was a cough, a whisper

and then

A LOUD HUSH.

At last a soft, blue glow lit the stage and the curtains twitched. ☛

WITH A RIPPLE OF GOLD BRAID. . . .

THE CURTAINS SLOWLY PARTED...

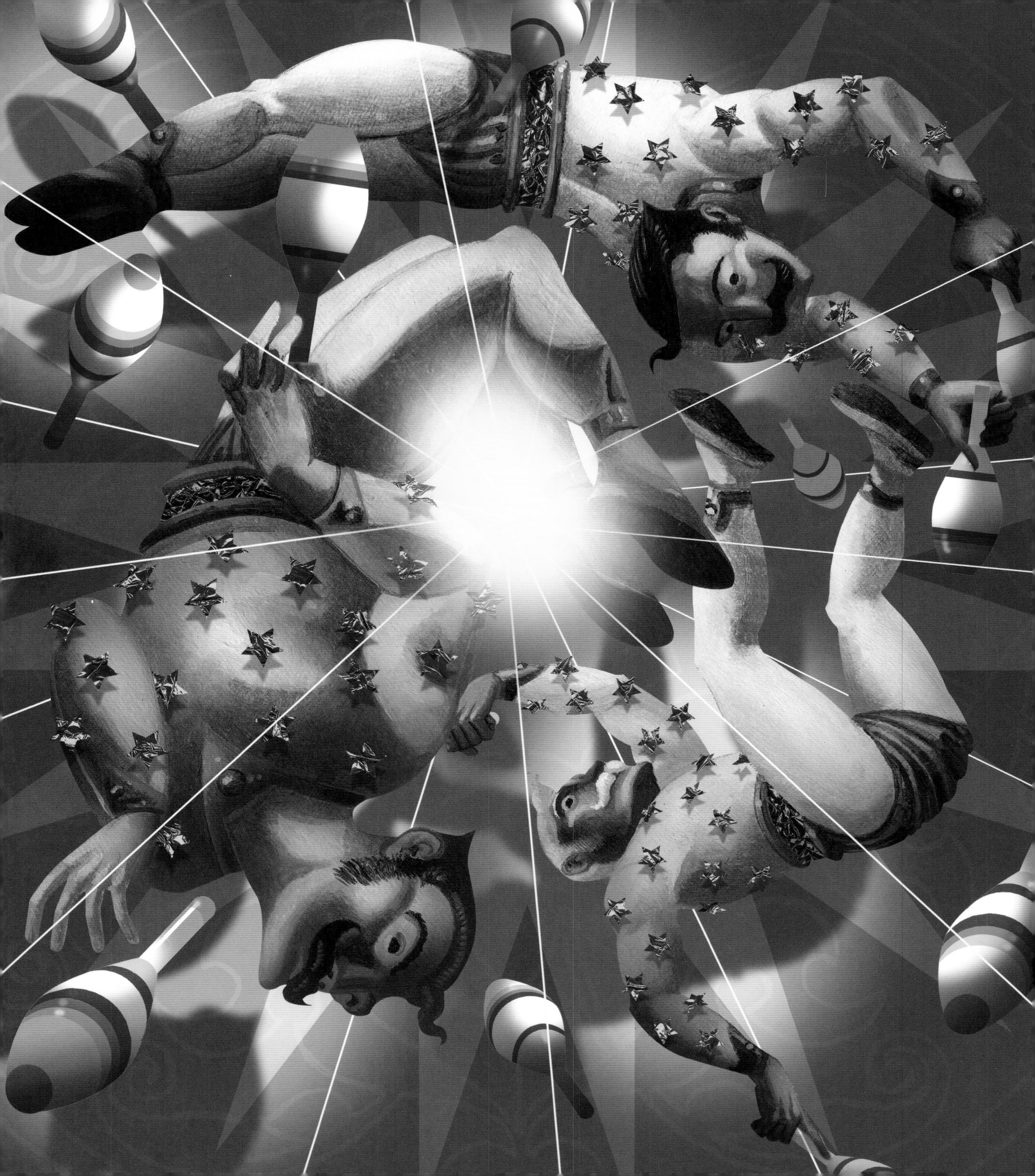

BANG!

THREE JUGGLERS

tumbled onto the stage to the pounding beat of a drum. Skittles flew, fast and furious, BACK AND FORTH, UP AND OVER. Tambourines rattled, loud and louder; skittles spun, high and higher; the jugglers twisted, fast and faster. THEN BANG THE SKITTLES WENT UP...

...but they didn't come down!

EVERYBODY CHEERED AND CLAPPED.

The jugglers bowed and bounced away.

ONCE MORE THERE WAS ONLY DARKNESS.

ArK

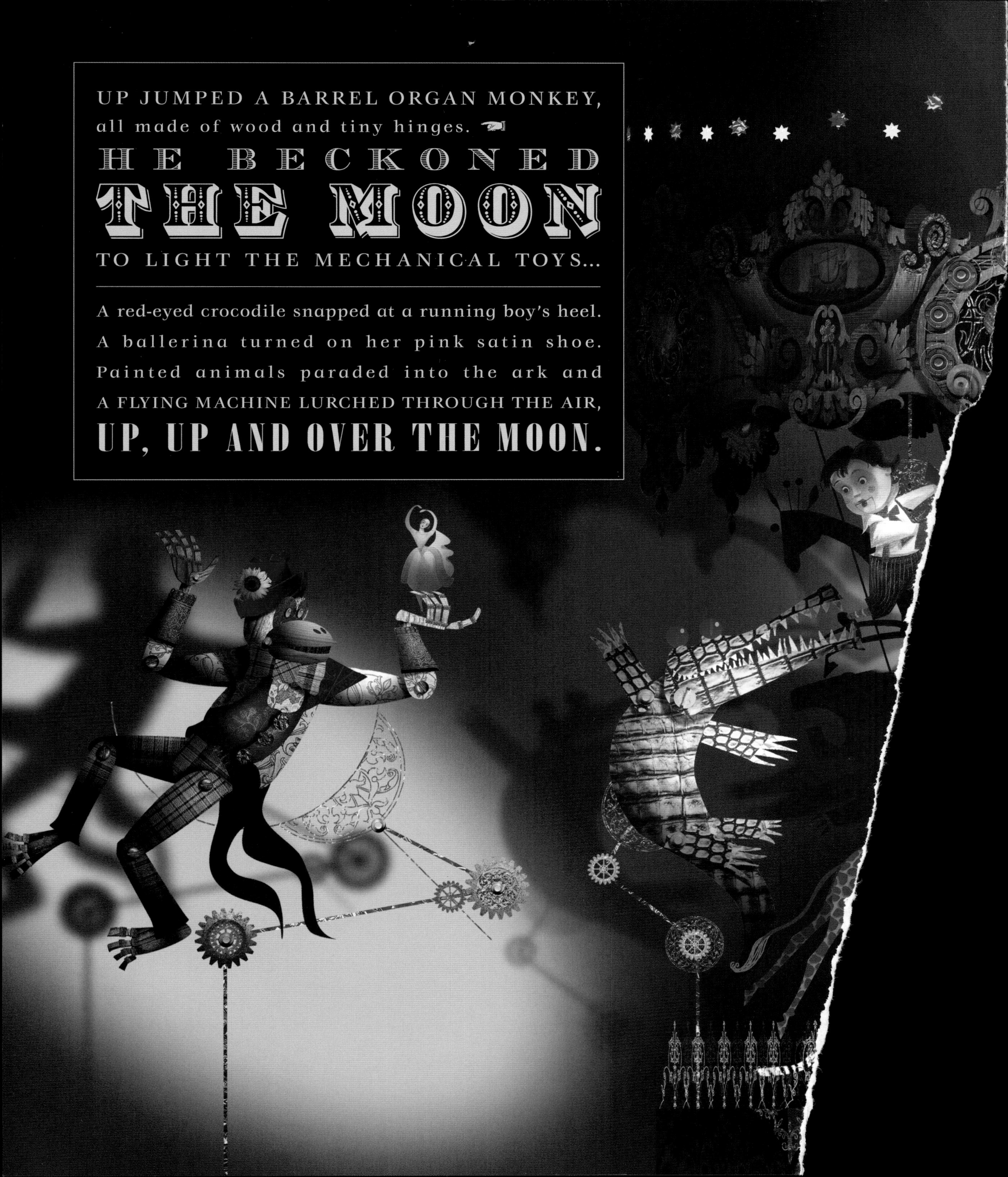

UP JUMPED A BARREL ORGAN MONKEY,
all made of wood and tiny hinges. ☛

HE BECKONED
THE MOON
TO LIGHT THE MECHANICAL TOYS...

A red-eyed crocodile snapped at a running boy's heel.
A ballerina turned on her pink satin shoe.
Painted animals paraded into the ark and
A FLYING MACHINE LURCHED THROUGH THE AIR,
UP, UP AND OVER THE MOON.

FOLD OUT ☞

NOW ONE DIM SPOTLIGHT
found a barrel organ, still and silent on the stage.

EVERYONE
HELD THEIR BREATH.

THE HANDLE BEGAN TO TURN
but there was no hand upon it. ☞

NOTE BY NOTE

the tinkling song of a carousel started
to dance from the pipes...

AT LAST THE BARREL ORGAN FELL SILENT.

NO ONE STIRRED.

For a moment the tiny creaks of the mechanical toys cast their own spell. Then they slowed, jerked awkwardly and were still.

THE SOLEMN MONKEY TOOK A STIFF BOW AND THE CURTAINS CLOSED TO LOUD APPLAUSE.

"NOW," SAID LEON, EDGING FORWARD IN THE DARK. "NOW IT'S GOING TO HAPPEN."

Outside in the night an owl hooted. With a swish THE CURTAINS OPENED...

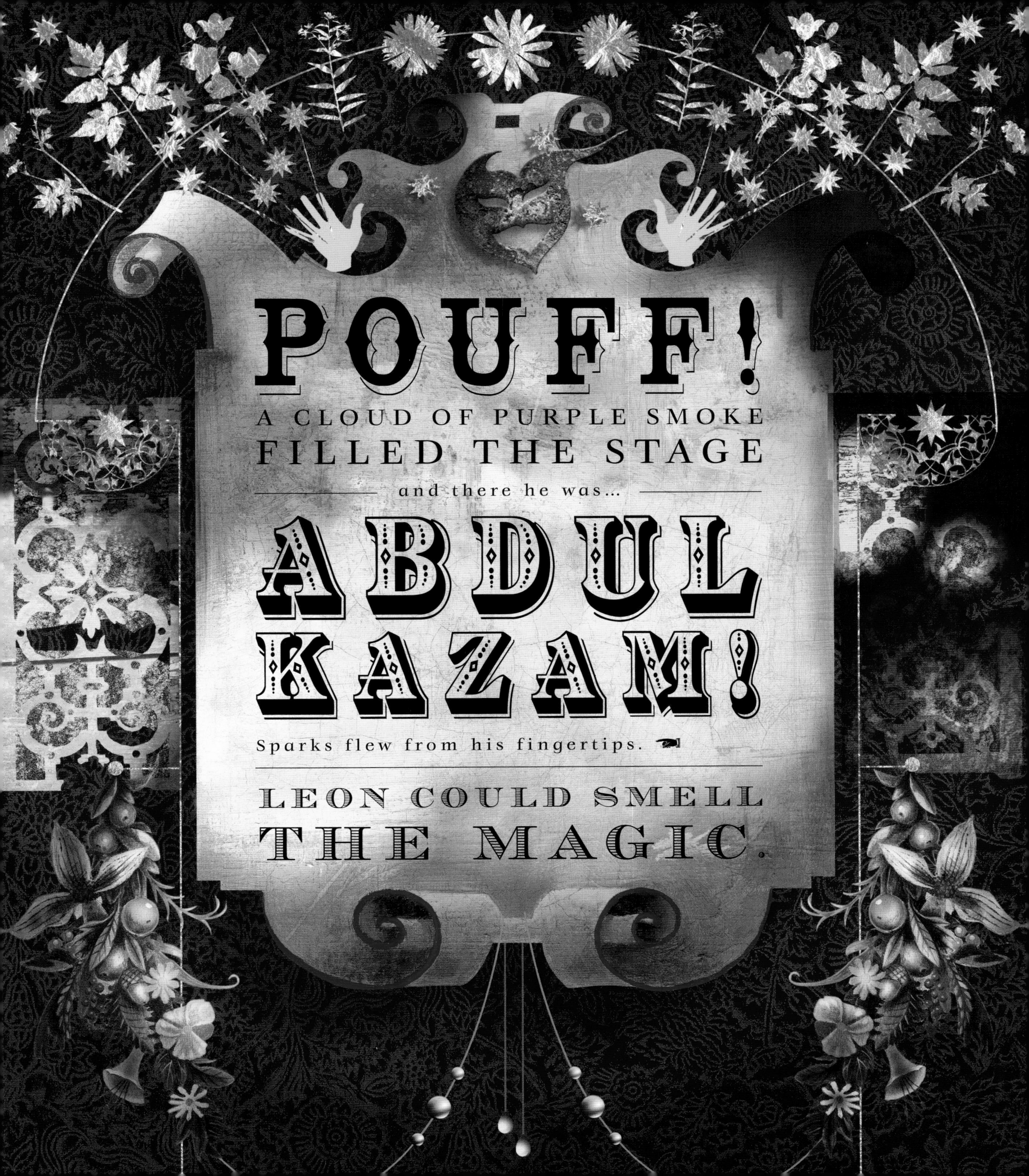
POUFF!
A CLOUD OF PURPLE SMOKE
FILLED THE STAGE
and there he was...
ABDUL
KAZAM!
Sparks flew from his fingertips.
LEON COULD SMELL
THE MAGIC.

"TRUST NOTHING..." SAID ABDUL KAZAM,
"BUT BELIEVE EVERYTHING!"

HE THREW HIS ARMS INTO THE AIR
AND THE MAGIC BEGAN.

PAPER FLOWERS BLOSSOMED FROM HIS SLEEVES; silk scarves changed colour at a whispered word; water, poured into a hat, turned into night air.

BRIGHT WHITE HANDKERCHIEFS
BECAME FLUTTERING DOVES.

The crowd was amazed. Then Abdul Kazam stepped aside and there was a door. A door into a box.

"WHO WILL STEP INTO THE MAGIC?"

LEON KNEW IT HAD TO BE HIM.

He stepped up to the stage and climbed INTO THE BOX.

There was a GASP from Little Mo and THE DOOR SHUT BEHIND HIM. ☛

INSIDE, the box was not a box. It was a world of doorways to Somewhere Else.
LEON fell down, down, down, until he tumbled onto a carpet.
"HELLO," said a boy in blue pantaloon trousers.
"Where am I?" asked LEON.
"This is THE PLACE BETWEEN," said the boy.
"Between WHAT?"
"Between there and back again. This is the place where MAGIC sends you."

"Will you show me?" asked LEON. The boy smiled. "Hold on tight."

He gave the carpet a tug. With a swoop, off they flew. Everything that disappeared by magic, appeared in the Place Between. Cards and doves fluttered in the lantern light. Coins and rings spun past, flashed and were gone. Ropes, cups and balls danced in the perfumed air. A magician's assistant stepped out of nowhere as another vanished in the blink of an eye! It was a world of astonishment. A world of the unexpected. It was alive with MAGIC.

The carpet came to rest. "Do you live here?" asked LEON, his eyes huge with wonder.

"No," said the boy. "But my father is a great magician. He makes me disappear every night. If I help him he will teach me magic."

Then LEON felt something soft wriggling behind him. A white rabbit climbed gently onto LEON's lap and nestled in his arms. The boy stroked her ears.

"She is always here," he said sadly. "She was never called back."

LEON hugged the lonely rabbit and gazed around the PLACE BETWEEN, enchanted and amazed.

Suddenly, the boy began to float away. "My father is calling," he said. "It is time to go."

LEON waved. "Goodbye," he cried. "I'll never forget!"

Then, from far away, he heard an echo of his own name.

"LEON, come back to us. **LEON, RETURN...**"

LEON felt the magic lift him off the ground and back into darkness.

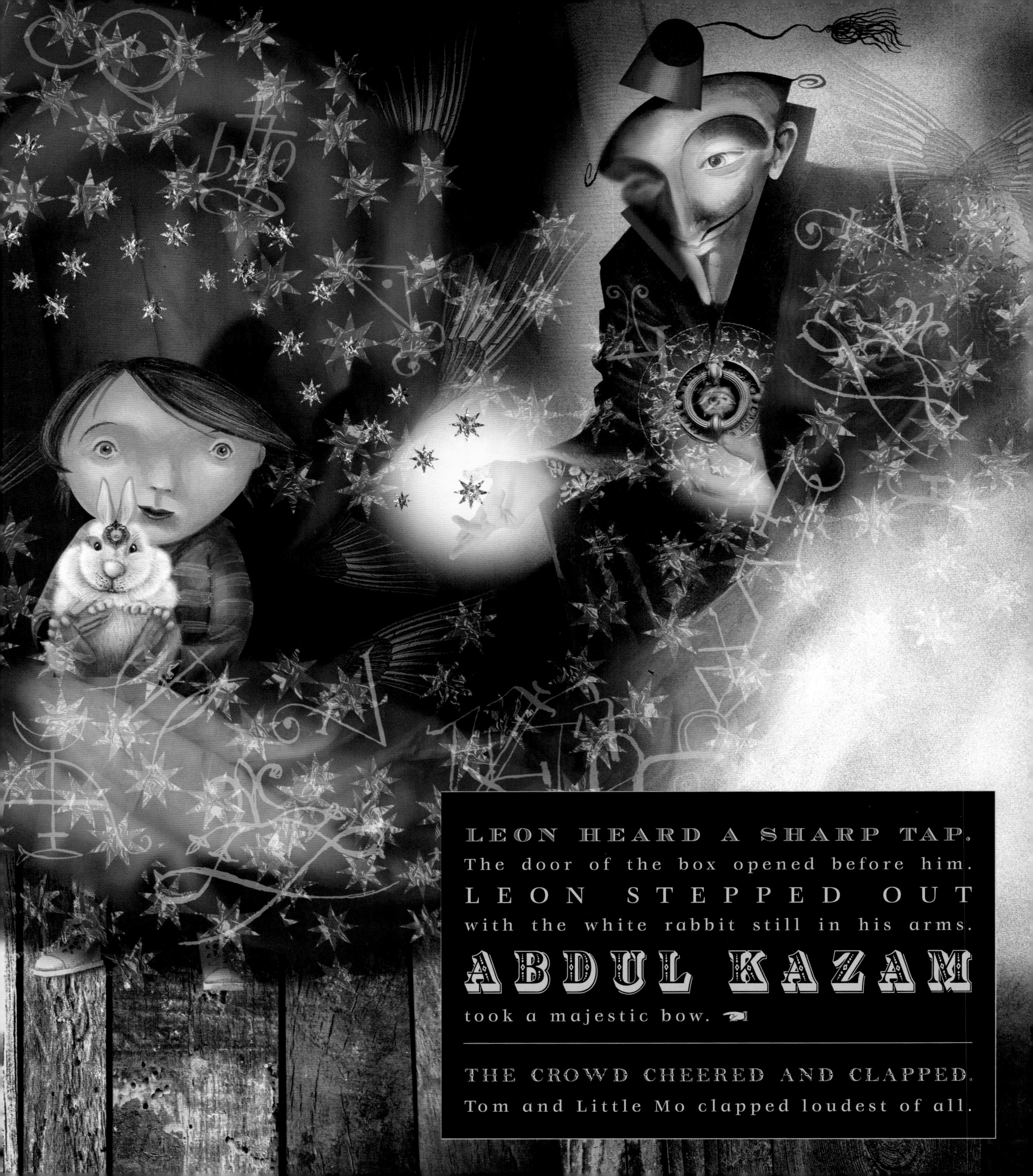

LEON HEARD A SHARP TAP.
The door of the box opened before him.
LEON STEPPED OUT
with the white rabbit still in his arms.
ABDUL KAZAM
took a majestic bow. ☛

THE CROWD CHEERED AND CLAPPED.
Tom and Little Mo clapped loudest of all.

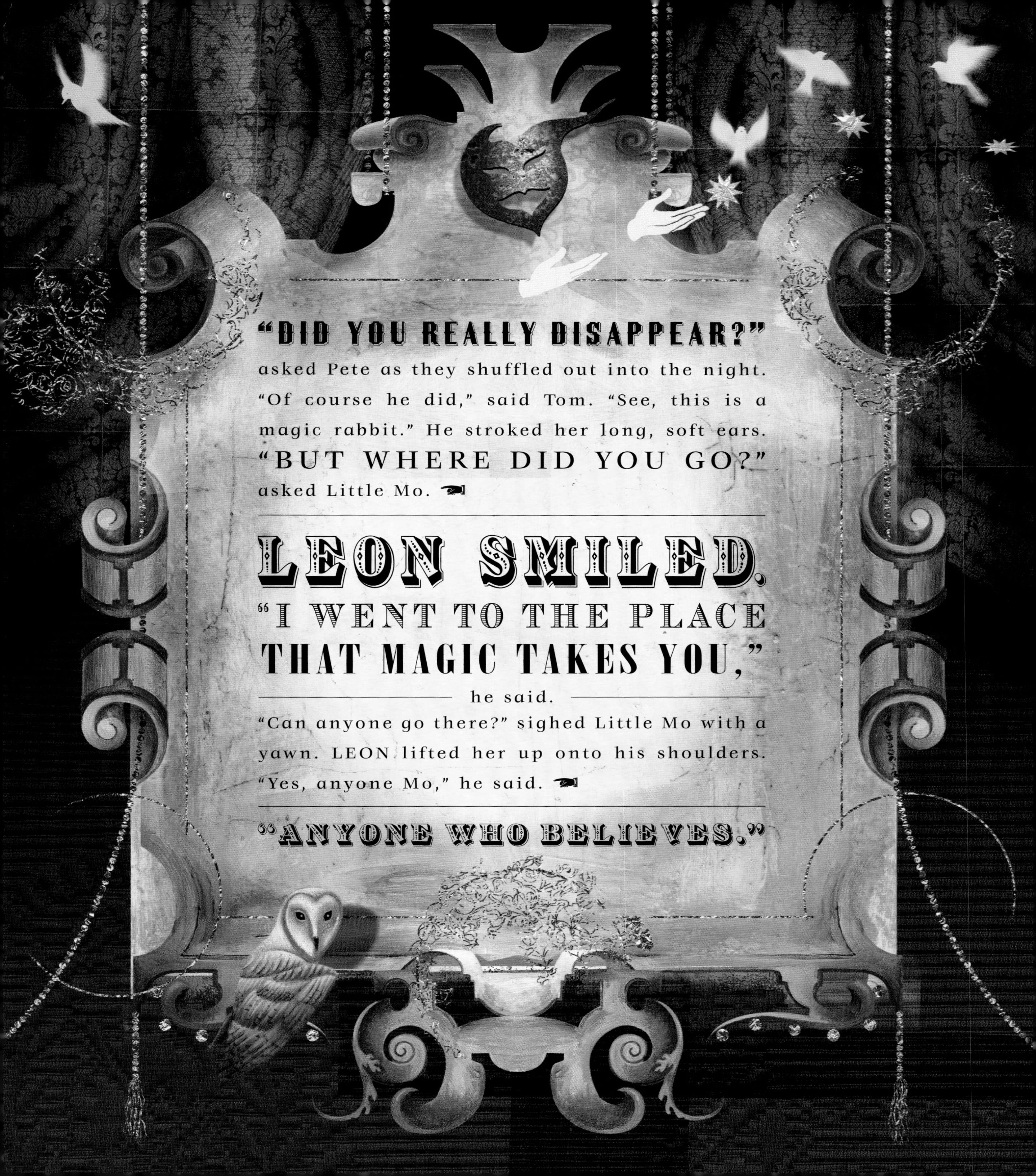
"DID YOU REALLY DISAPPEAR?"
asked Pete as they shuffled out into the night.
"Of course he did," said Tom. "See, this is a magic rabbit." He stroked her long, soft ears.
"BUT WHERE DID YOU GO?"
asked Little Mo. ▶
LEON SMILED.
"I WENT TO THE PLACE THAT MAGIC TAKES YOU,"
he said.
"Can anyone go there?" sighed Little Mo with a yawn. LEON lifted her up onto his shoulders.
"Yes, anyone Mo," he said. ▶
"ANYONE WHO BELIEVES."

MAGIC
SHOW
TONIGHT

A TEMPLAR BOOK

FIRST PUBLISHED IN THE UK BY TEMPLAR PUBLISHING, AN IMPRINT OF
THE TEMPLAR COMPANY PLC,
THE GRANARY, NORTH STREET, DORKING, SURREY, RH4 1DN, UK
WWW.TEMPLARCO.CO.UK

FIRST EDITION

ISBN 978-1-84011-801-8

DESIGNED BY MIKE JOLLEY
EDITED BY LIBBY HAMILTON

PRINTED IN CHINA